GLAD TO BE A GIRL

Jacquelyn Craighead
Art by Gary D. Sanchez

Xulon Press

Xulon Press
2301 Lucien Way #415
Maitland, FL 32751
407.339.4217
www.xulonpress.com

© 2022 by Jacquelyn Craighead

Paperback ISBN-13: 978-1-66284-552-9
Hard Cover ISBN-13: 978-1-66284-553-6
Ebook ISBN-13: 978-1-66284-554-3

Dedicated to: Every girl - Everywhere

Special Thanks to:
Karen, Kimberly, Dana, Alena,
and a group of grown girls!

GLAD TO BE A GIRL

I'm glad to be a girl
and a girl I will be
but
that doesn't mean
I can't climb a big tree!

glad To BE A giRl

I'm glad to be a girl
and a girl I will be!
Being dainty is fun
but
that doesn't mean
I don't like to run.

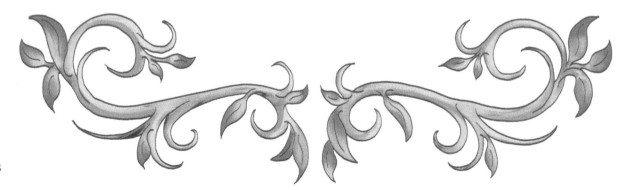

glad To BE A girl

I'm glad to be a girl
and a girl I will be!
I adore dance class and tutus
but
that doesn't mean I can't play with choo-choos.

glad to be a girl

I'm glad to be a girl
and a girl I will be!
I love reading girly stories
and exploring in a laboratory.

glad To BE A giRl

I'm glad to be a girl
and a girl I will be
but
I love watching boys play
because they are so different from me!

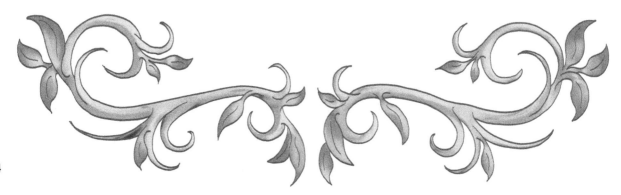

BOYS SAY FUNNY THINGS

Boys say funny things
and do silly tricks,
while I sit and pout
because I'm too young for lipstick!

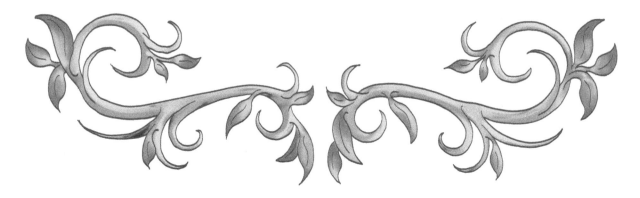

GiRLS CAN ENjoy THiNGS

Girls can enjoy things done easily by boys
without her forsaking
the body of her making!

CREATED TO BE A GIRL

I was created to be a girl
and a girl I will be
a precious, unique pearl
born into this wide world.

CREATED TO BE A GIRL

I was created to be a girl
and a girl I will be!
God made me a girl
for all eternity!

CPSIA information can be obtained
at www.ICGtesting.com
Printed in the USA
JSHW011317150522
25693JS00009B/9